JOY SPARTON
and the
MYSTERY IN ROOM 7

by

RUTH I. JOHNSON

moody press
chicago

Printed in the United States of America

Contents

CHAPTER		PAGE
1.	The Prospect of Sam	5
2.	Police Raid	15
3.	Room Change	26
4.	New House, New Problems	34
5.	An Unexpected Encounter	42
6.	The Suspicious Mr. Sinkey	50
7.	Too Much Imagination?	57
8.	An Invitation to Stay	68
9.	Two Empty Seats	76
10.	Nabbed by the Police	83
11.	Sam Comes Clean	89

1

The Prospect of Sam

WE HAD LIVED on Parsonage Hill so long that, when Dad finally decided to accept the call from the church in Lake Port, I started to get a sick feeling in my stomach. Roy and I were only about two years old when we moved here, so somehow I guess I just thought we would live here forever.

If Dad had asked me today what I thought about his accepting the new church, I probably would have told him that I didn't think it was God's will for us to leave Parsonage Hill. But you might know, Dad talked it over with God, not with me. I'm pretty sure Dad thought God was a whole lot more reliable than his very own daughter. And since this next Sunday was going to be our last Sunday here, I guess it was pretty obvious that God must have told Dad it was OK to leave.

Now that it was so close, I decided maybe I should have talked to God about it too—more than I had. I could have told Him that it would be better for us to stay here a little longer. When I got to thinking about leaving Susan and some of my other friends, boy, I really felt terrible. And then there was David Tanner. For all the years I had known him, he had only thought of me as Roy's twin sister. And now that we were leaving, his eyes must have been getting much better, because lately he treated me like I was a girl, not like Roy's dumb sister.

"How can Dad be so sure that we should go to Lake Port?" I asked my mother, while we were stacking the dinner dishes.

"Because he feels God is leading us there."

I knew she'd give me that kind of an answer. Somehow a preacher's wife, even though she is your mother, always comes through with a spiritual answer to all your not-so-spiritual questions.

"Would it matter to Dad if I thought maybe God was telling us to stay here a little longer?" I finally dared to ask the question that had been on my mind the whole time. I don't suppose I really thought God was telling us to stay. I guess what I was trying to figure out was a way to convince God that it was OK to stay. Didn't He know that all my friends were here, that I really didn't want to move?

I remembered all the times that I heard Dad preach about knowing God's will and being obedient when He told us to do something or go some-where. Dad always used the story about Abraham being willing to give up his son if that's what God wanted.

And I really knew that I couldn't just pray and tell God how He should lead us. But oh, how I hated to leave the only home I could ever remember.

Mother must have known how I felt, because all of a sudden she got terribly serious.

"Why, Honey, you know that Daddy and I prayed about it for a long time, and we talked to you and Roy, too. Why didn't you say something about it earlier?"

I opened my mouth to answer the question but even before one word popped out, Roy came through with his smart answer.

"She didn't realize it would mean leaving David Tanner. It just dawned on her now."

I grabbed the dish towel, whipped it over at Roy, but missed him completely. It was OK for me to think about David. But Roy? Did he have to say such a stupid thing right in front of Mother?

Either Mother wasn't listening, or she decided to ignore Roy's bright comment. I think she felt it was more important to explain to me about God telling us that He had a new place of service for Dad.

"Joy, when God leads, it's for us to follow, not ask why. Evidently our ministry here is over."

Boy, with that kind of an answer, how could I say why again!

But these were the bare facts: I'd have to be going to a brand new school and since Lake Port was bigger, I'd probably feel awful lonely there. I knew I would especially dread the first day.

Then too, I'd have to find all new friends. I knew one thing for sure, I'd never find as good a friend as Susan Tanner.

"I wonder if God would ever lead the Tanners to Lake Port?" I asked, hardly realizing that I had said it out loud.

Before Mother could tell me that it wasn't likely that God would tell Mr. Tanner to pack up his business and follow us to our new church, Roy butted in again.

"Hey, I know! God could tell David Tanner to propose to you, and you could be a child bride and live happily ever after."

"Roy," Mother said, a shocked look on her face. I was surprised she didn't scold him about being sacrilegious.

I could have slapped my brother right across his

8

talkative mouth, but instead I glared like I'd never glared before.

"Nobody asked you for your smart remark," I snapped. "Anyway, I don't think you want to move any more than I do."

"I think moving is neato. Maybe there'll be a chance to get into sports in Lake Port. Here it's all sewed up."

"Sports! That's all you ever think of."

"Sure, that's life."

"Life? That's stupid."

"Children!" Mother finally said.

I knew, if we kept at it long enough, Mother would step in as a referee. She always did.

"Let's not fight about things that haven't even happened yet," she added. "It would be a great deal better if you would go upstairs and start packing some of your things. It has to be done and today's as good a day as any to start."

"But we don't move until Wednesday," Roy argued.

Now it was my turn.

"So some of the things will be in a box for a few extra days. Big deal!"

Roy looked at me as if to say none of your business, and he probably would have except that Dad walked in just then with the morning mail.

"Anything for me?" I asked.

"Nope." Roy put in before Dad could answer. "David can't write until we move."

Neither Dad nor Mother saw the face I made at him. They were too interested in an airmail letter that was in the stack.

"Oh. From Carl and Ethel," Mother said, eagerly opening the envelope.

"Let me have the stamp," Roy said, jumping up, trying to grab the letter that had come from South America.

Mother jerked it away just as fast, and Dad started toward the door, looking over some of the other mail.

"I wonder what they have to say?" Mother asked no one in particular. Dad stopped in his tracks and raised his eyebrows.

"If you read it, I think you'll find out." He spoke soft, like he wasn't sure he wanted Mother to hear him. But she did, and now it was Mother's turn to pass out the dirty looks. If Dad hadn't been checking another letter, he would have seen that it wasn't exactly a preacher's-wife look that she gave him either.

"Oh my," Mother said as she started reading. That's how she usually reacted when something bad was about to happen.

Dad must have thought she was about to faint or something because he came dashing back to the table. Well, dashing for Dad. For anyone else it would have been sauntering.

"What's the matter?" he asked, speaking louder than he had before.

"Sam. They want to know if Sam can come and live with us this next school year."

"Neato!" was Roy's reaction.

Dad took the letter from Mother and at the same time turned and looked at Roy.

"Would you please stop using that ridiculous word."

"Neato?"

"Yes. Neato." Daddy said with a harshness that he didn't often use.

"What's wrong with neato?"

Neither Mom nor Dad answered his question so I felt I should take care of it.

"It's a stupid word, that's what it is."

"Stupid!" Roy pounced back. "You use *that* dumb word all the time. So what's the difference?"

11

"Well, you say, 'dumb.' "

By this time we had Mom and Dad's attention again.

"Children!"

When Dad said, "children" that way, it really meant, "Button up now before I do the buttoning for you."

He turned back to the letter.

"Hm. Carl actually wrote this time. He must be pretty concerned about it."

"That's probably because Sam's a backslider," I blurted out.

"Joy," Dad replied, "You shouldn't call your cousin a backslider."

"Well, he is. He's—and anyway you use that word in the pulpit."

"Joy!" It was Mother's turn to chime in this time, and then with hardly a breath she started reading the letter aloud.

" 'And so we are very concerned that we have Sam in school and settled in a good Christian home before we go back into the interior.' "

"See, I told you he was a backslider. Even Uncle Carl knows it."

"Oh my," Mother managed again. "Moving to a new place and then taking on a boy like—" She stopped suddenly. Either she would have to admit that Sam wasn't exactly the kind of Christian he ought to be, or she would have to stop short. She stopped short.

So I finished her sentence with a question.

"A backslider, Mom?"

Without answering, Mom and Dad took off for the study, and Roy and I started talking about how things would be if Sam came to live with us.

"I think it'd be neat to have Sam here."

"Don't you mean it would be 'neato'?" I said with sarcasm.

"Okay, neato!"

"I agree with Dad. That word sounds stupid."

"You haven't answered my question. Do you think it'll be good or bad to have Sam here?" Roy was serious as he spoke this time.

"I don't know. A new church, new friends, a new school—and Sam too?"

Roy whistled like he suddenly got the point.

"Come to think of it, it would be a rotten way to start a new school. Having your wild cousin set the reputation for you."

That really made me think. Just because he was a missionary's son didn't mean he had to be a good Christian, and just because Roy and I were preacher's kids didn't mean that we would be good Christians either. Everyone had the same responsibilities. God expected us to be good Christians, but He always let us choose. He never forced us to live a certain way.

These weren't really my own thoughts. I had heard Dad preach like that. What Roy was saying was true. Sam's testimony and life would sure make things hard on us at school. But there was something even more important—what would it do for Dad and a brand-new church?

kids didn't mean that we would be good Christians either. Everyone had the same responsibilities. God expected us to be good Christians, but Heaven was for no-one. He expected us to be good Christians for Him no matter what... He wanted us to

2

Police Raid

MOVING DAY, ugh! Especially the way Mother does it. After everything had been packed and the movers had finally gone, we had to stay and scrub every inch of the house from the top of the ceiling right to the floor—and the floor too.

I couldn't figure out why that had to be done now. We were leaving it. Who would know if there was a speck of dust left in the corner? When I mentioned that, Mom kept saying God would know how we left it and so would the new minister's wife. Right at that very second my tongue was all ready to ask if she was more worried about God or what the new minister's wife would think. But the more I thought about it, the more I decided that was exactly the question I should not ask right then.

"I refuse to leave this house like a pigpen," Mother said, letting her eyes scan the empty rooms.

For an answer Dad only snorted.

15

I had to smile too, but I didn't laugh out loud. If our house was a pigpen, some pig sure would have a hard time finding a speck of dust, let alone some mud to roll in. Mother was one of those who cleaned so often she practically wore out the carpet. She wouldn't even let a thread stay on the floor for more than a second. She'd get up from the table or from her reading or anything just to pick it up. So I knew our house just couldn't have been a very good place for a pig. But when Mom said scrub, we scrubbed— all four of us. At least for once Dad and Roy found out what it was like to get down on their knees for something other than devotions.

With all this cleaning going on, I just kept waiting for either Dad or Mother to use it as a sermon illustration. Even though Mother wasn't the preacher, she sometimes came up with better illustrations than Dad did.

And one of them was sure to say, "This is just like the spiritual life." That's the way they usually started when they wanted us to give them our attention. So since I was thinking of it this time, I thought it wouldn't be too bad if I would say it.

"This is just like the Christian life," I said, changing it just a little. The minute I said those words everyone looked up at me like what had ever inspired *her* to come up with such a good statement. Boy, was everyone listening now!

"Dad preaches that, even though we go to church and read our Bibles and pray and everything," I said, "every now and then we have to have revival meetings to get us thinking about the little dirty corners in our life."

The minute I finished saying that line, I knew I had said the right thing. Dad looked at me like everything was just about perfect, and even Mother smiled like she was pleased. Roy didn't exactly smile, but then he never did smile at me too often. I guess brothers don't try to be friendly with sisters.

"That's right," Roy said, not wanting to sound any less spiritual than I did. "We wash our hands and face every day, and we still have to take a bath."

If the conversation had not been getting so serious I would probably have said, "Yes, but you sure try to get out of it every chance you get." But somehow I didn't think this was the time to say anything so unkind.

Instead, I said, "I suppose you can think of house-cleaning like the house is having a revival." Mother wasn't sure the comparison was right, but she said if it helped me to think about my own spiritual life, it was OK to think of the house having a revival.

As usual, Roy thought my idea was dumb.

I knew the first thing we would be doing at the new house was to help it have a revival too. Again, I couldn't really see why. Because if the lady who had lived there didn't want the next minister's wife to—oh well, I knew it would be just as well to plan to scrub and get it over with. But at least I wouldn't have to worry about that for a couple of days. We were going to stay in a motel tonight since the moving van would not get there with our furniture until morning.

Our last night at church was really terrible. People had forgotten all about those times I had caused so much trouble—the times before I was a Christian and even once in a while when I hadn't let Jesus Christ control my life.

The church people looked so sad. I knew one thing for sure, the first day at the new house we would have to do a whole washer full of hankies. Boy, did Mom ever go through a batch of them!

I wanted to sneak out of the service and the reception, but David Tanner was there and I was not going to miss one single second of seeing him before we left. He told me he would write and that we would see each other at Bible camp next year, but oh, man, that seemed like forever right then. In fact, we had only been back from camp a few weeks as it was.

Finally we were sitting in the car, almost ready to take off. Then without any notice whatsoever, like saying, "Let's pray," Dad started right out with, "Dear heavenly Father." That hushed us in a hurry. He usually gave us some kind of warning that it was time to bow our heads and stuff, but here he started right in without an announcement or anything.

We were all talking when he started, but it got terribly quiet when he paused. Suddenly it dawned on me that his voice had cracked right in the middle of "heavenly," almost like Roy's voice does every now and then.

With that crack in Dad's voice, Mom had made a wild dive for her purse, pulled out a hankie and started blowing again. There had been more nose blowing in our church last Sunday than I had ever remembered. It had been bad enough when all the speeches were made. But oh, wow, you should have heard what was going on during, "God Be with You Till We Meet Again." You never heard so much coughing and blowing from one congregation. If I hadn't known better, I would have thought that our choir director had given the signal: one, two, three, blow! And here in the car it looked like Mom was going to start up again.

"We will be eternally grateful," Dad was praying, ignoring all the sniffling and stuff from Mom, "for the years we have had here." By now he had gone into his preacher's voice. "We thank Thee for those who have come to know Jesus Christ as Saviour." And then just as though God didn't remember who they were, Dad started mentioning a bunch of the people by name. And Mom grabbed another hankie.

"We think especially of our dear friends Mr. and Mrs. Tanner and Susan and David."

And at the mention of David's name, I wondered if Dad had any idea what a dear friend I thought David was. I wondered too if I would ever see him again. He had promised to write to me, but at this moment I wasn't sure he really meant it.

I wondered how old I would be before I got to thinking about marriage. Mother told me about her cousin who had liked a boy in junior high school and ended up marrying him.

Maybe someday David Tanner and I would be married. After all, David was a Christian and that's the thing that Dad and Mother had always told us— only to go with Christians, because someday we would want to get married and we had to be sure that they belonged to the Lord like we did.

I remember hearing Dad pray with some people for a life's partner, but somehow it didn't exactly seem like I should pray for a life's partner right now. I wasn't even sure I ever wanted to get married. Maybe I would end up being an explorer or a scientist or something else instead.

While my mind was wandering, Dad must have still been praying. I don't know what other names he mentioned to God because I had stopped short with David Tanner. I must have been thinking about him for a long time because Dad's prayers aren't usually too short and all at once he was saying, "We commit to Thee this trip and ourselves, trusting Thee for guidance, and protection. In Jesus' name, Amen."

By the time we got out of town Mom had sort of settled down and I almost spoiled it by bringing up some things that had happened on one of our vacations.

"Dad, do you remember the time I was supposed to find the route for you on the map, and instead I picked those little numbers that tell how many miles it is between cities?"

Dad remembered, and so did Roy.

"Man, were you ever stupid," he said. "Anybody who doesn't know what a route on a map looks like ought to be committed."

Dad must have thought it was a good time to make a point too.

"And because that wasn't too many years ago and because we're on that same road, I don't believe I'll rely on you for help on this trip."

I would have commented, but Roy was still going.

"Man, that was a neat vacation. Remember the snakes that got into our cabin?"

"And that little girl who was lost in the woods."

That started Mother to blubber again and for a minute I thought we were going to have a second verse to the nose blowing song that we had last Sunday night.

"And we will long thank God for all the good years," Dad interjected. "And press toward the mark of the high calling of Christ Jesus." He was using his preacher's voice again.

Roy and I looked at each other because usually when Dad started quoting a Scripture, it meant that some special point was to be made for our good. But nothing came. Dad must just have been thinking of the new work that God had called him to go to.

"When is Sam coming?" I asked, deciding it was a good time to change the subject.

Mom came through with her typical, "Oh, my. Did you have to bring that up right now?"

So Dad took over.

"We wired Uncle Carl last night and suggested they could just as well come this weekend. I gave them our new address and directions on catching a bus to Lake Port from the international airport."

"Carl and Ethel and Sam here on our first weekend and we won't even be settled," Mother mumbled, but Dad still heard it.

"It was now or never," he said. "If Sam doesn't come now, he won't get started with school in time."

Mother didn't say it, but I'll bet anything she was thinking "never" would sure be a lot better.

For a minute I was sorry I had brought up the subject of Sam.

Dad and Mom had promised both God and Uncle Carl that Sam could live with us this next year, but they sure seemed nervous about it. Even though they would not call him a backslider, I was sure they knew he wasn't really living for the Lord or at least not as close as they always wanted us to live. Maybe they were wondering if Sam's bad influence would rub off on Roy and me.

When we finally arrived at the motel where we were to stay that night, we found it had an oval-shaped swimming pool and a beautiful white lattice balcony. I kept waiting for Roy to pop off with "neato," but he must have forgotten that this was his favorite word. Either that or his mind was on the three police cars that were parked by the door right next to the room that had been assigned to us.

Roy came through with another remark instead. "Hey Dad, whatcha been doing? They finally caught up with you."

But Dad didn't laugh. Instead his eyes were moving back and forth from the police cars to the other officers who were standing in a huddle. Two policemen stood on each side of the room entrance while another one took out his gun, pointed it in the direction of the motel door. He knocked loudly and called out, "Police. Open up."

"Oh, my," Mom said pathetically. "Whatever is going on? Why would God lead us to something like this?"

I glanced over at her, still looking toward room number seven. I wanted to remind her about the sermon she had given me just the other day when I asked why God would lead us away from Parsonage Hill—and David Tanner. But I decided not to say anything. Actually, I was asking myself the same question.

We had just arrived in the city where our new church was, where Roy and I would soon be going to a new school, where Sam was coming to live. And the first thing we see is a police raid.

What in the world were we getting into?

3

Room Change

WE WERE SO STUNNED by what we saw that we weren't even able to get out of the car. Dad sat staring, first at the blue police cars and then at room number seven, realizing how close all this was to our own motel door. I sort of hoped Dad wouldn't make us get out right now. In a way, I didn't want to miss anything that was going on; and in a way, I was much too scared to move.

"That cop's got a gun," Roy said.

"Oh my," Mom said for about the fourth time since we had pulled up to the motel. I think Mom would have given most anything right then to be back on Parsonage Hill. And I felt the same way. In fact, I would even have volunteered to do all the scrubbing in our old home.

After knocking again and receiving no answer, one of the policemen kicked the door open with his foot, and all of the other officers rushed into the room with one big force. It was just the way I had seen it on some of the television programs that Dad told us not to watch, the ones we had sneaked a peek at when the folks were out. But this wasn't television; it was real action with real police. And Dad was not able to tell us to turn it off.

As the police rushed into the room, I closed my eyes, expecting any minute to hear gunshots. Instead there was a deafening stillness. Even Roy wasn't spouting off about anything. In just a few minutes, the police officers came marching out of the room and got back into their cars.

"Hey, Dad!" Roy shouted. "Let's go over and ask them what happened."

"Don't you dare leave us alone." Mom's voice was hoarse with panic, as though she fully expected to see Dad and Roy walk over to the police cars.

Dad looked over at her and patted her on the arm.

"Well, whatever they were looking for, they obviously didn't find it."

"That only means something is still wrong," Mom added.

As soon as the police cars began to pull away, we got out of the car and Dad unlocked the door to our motel room.

All the time I was standing there, I kept wondering if maybe the police had the wrong room and, when we unlocked ours, a bunch of tough-looking guys would come flying out, running toward us with guns and things. And Mom must have been worried about the same thing. As I turned to see what she was doing, I saw her bending over some pieces of luggage in the car—luggage she knew very well Roy and Dad would be taking into the room. Every now and then she would look up to see if there was anyone coming out of our motel room.

Dad saw what Mom was doing, too.

"It's all clear, Dear," he called, a chuckle in his voice. "You can come out now."

As Dad was talking with Mom, Roy's eyes were trying to follow the direction that the police cars had gone.

"I wonder if you and I ought to go around and ask the manager what's going on, Dad?"

"You will stay right here with me—us," Mother said, a worried look on her face.

Roy winked at Dad. "Well, don't you think we ought to go to the office and get a newspaper or something? After all, if we're going to live in this town we ought to know something about it."

Dad knew what Roy was trying to do, but in order

not to frighten Mother any more than she was, he just said, "Maybe later."

Mother was opening all the different doors in our room, almost expecting someone to come jumping out of one of them.

"Whatever does this door lead to?" she asked, opening it just a crack.

"That is known as a bathroom," Dad said coldly.

"Oh, I thought the bath and shower were over there," Mother said, pointing to another door.

"They call that a closet," Roy added, enjoying the fact that Mother was so upset.

"Honey, I don't think you have to be frightened any longer," Dad said. "If there was any danger, the police would not have left. Try to relax."

But Mom didn't seem to hear anything Dad was saying.

"This is a terrible way to start life in a new city," she said, "I do hope this is no sign of things to come."

Roy was still enjoying the whole thing.

"Well, if the city is so evil, they can come to our church and hear a good preacher tell them how to change their wicked ways!"

Roy meant it as a joke, but nobody laughed.

Even though Dad had told Mom to relax, neither he nor Mom looked as though they were enjoying the evening. I think if there had been a blast of any kind outside, everyone of us, including my mouthy twin brother, would have slid under the bed just about as fast as possible.

"Well," Dad finally said, "I'm glad Carl and Ethel aren't here yet. If they had seen this, I'm not too sure they would have been willing to leave their wayward son in a city like this."

I was shocked. This was the first time Dad had admitted that Sam had a spiritual problem. He wouldn't let us say that word *backslider*, but the word *wayward* seemed to be okay.

I knew when we had devotions later in the evening Dad would be praying for Uncle Carl and Aunt Ethel. He would be telling God to use us to help Sam become a better Christian. I was pretty sure he wouldn't use the word *backslide*, but he would probably say, "Draw Sam to Thyself." I wasn't exactly sure what that meant. It seemed to me it was easier to say, "God, Sam isn't living for You. So please make him come back and be a good Christian again."

But Dad didn't pray that way. He prayed with Bible verses and words that sounded like Dad, not like me. And I guess that's what God wants us to do—pray like we feel.

I knew too that he would want to be sure to tell

God thanks for taking care of us on the trip. We hadn't even had a flat tire this time. And even though I wasn't too excited about finding the police right outside of our motel door, we had gotten here without any trouble, and we really weren't in any trouble now. We were safe in the motel, and nothing bad had happened.

Mother had just opened one of the smaller suitcases and was about to pull out a dress when there was a knock at the door.

"Don't answer it!" She practically screamed it out.

Dad got up from his chair, walked toward the door and said, "Of course we have to answer it."

"But it might be those—those people the police are looking for."

"Yeah, and it might be the cops to come and get Dad," Roy added. All along his voice seemed to be saying, "I hope it is something exciting."

When Dad finally got the door unlocked and opened, there stood the motel manager.

"Reverend Sparton?" he asked, just as though he didn't know, even though that was the name Dad had signed when he registered.

"Yes."

"I wonder if you and your family would mind if we gave you another room?"

31

Dad looked at the man just as if to say, "There's nothing wrong with this room." Instead he said nothing.

By this time Mom had gone to the door, too.

"Whatever for?" she asked. And she didn't use that preacher's-wife tone that she used when she met important people.

"Well, I understand you're to be the new preacher at Community Church," he said with a big smile. All of us knew he was just giving us a line. "We'd like to offer you a suite instead of this room."

"Thank you," Dad said. "That isn't necessary. This room is perfectly all right for one evening."

The manager cleared his throat; and, when he spoke again, there was an urgent sound to his voice.

"Sir, may I suggest that you accept our offer of another room."

"The cops want this one?" Roy blurted out.

A look of shock came over the manager's face.

Dad saw there was something bothering the man and lowered his voice. "We saw what happened next door," he said. "Is there some sort of problem?"

"I'm not at liberty to give you any information, Reverend," the manager said. "I only came to offer you another room."

"Thank you," Dad said. "We'll be glad to move if you'll just tell us where you want us to go."

With that, Mother shook her head and began packing the dress back into the suitcase. The manager came into our room, picked up a couple of the suitcases, and told Dad to drive the car around to the other side.

"Room eighteen," he said. "It's all ready for you."

As Dad got into the car, Mother, Roy, and I followed the man to the opposite side of the building. Passing the room marked "Office," we looked in and saw two policemen leaning on the counter.

"I knew it," Roy shouted. "I knew it. They're waiting to take our room. Something's still fishy around here."

The manager did not answer. Instead he hurried past the office and on to room eighteen. Nervously he put the key into the lock, still looking around, almost expecting something dramatically unusual to happen.

4

New House, New Problems

DAD AND MOM didn't say they were worried, but I could tell. Like Roy and me, they were expecting something to happen too.

I guess I was sort of waiting for some shots, some loud talking, or something that would sound like there was a lot of trouble. But instead, it turned out to be one long quiet night. And by morning all of us looked like we had hardly slept—and we hadn't.

There was a pizza place right across the street from the motel, and Roy and I thought that, since we hadn't slept too much, pizza would help to make us a little more sharp. But somehow Dad and Mother didn't feel that would be a good breakfast. We even voted on where to go—Mom and Dad voted for an eggs and bacon place, and Roy and I took the pizza house. But even though the voting came out even, guess where we didn't go? That's the way it is with adults. They let you vote, and then they go and do things the way they had planned the whole time anyway. But I suppose in this case it was OK since Dad was the one who was going to pay. Then too, he had called a man from the church to tell him where we'd be.

When we got to the café, Dr. Becker, the man from the church, was waiting at the entrance. Dad introduced us; and from then on he and Dad talked up a storm, hardly even including Mom in the conversation. It was clear that Roy and I were definitely left out, so we took up our own subject.

We weren't thinking of Dr. Becker or church or breakfast or anything. I knew what I was thinking, and I found out Roy had the same thing on his mind. We were still over at the motel—and not in our new room either.

Without telling Roy that I was thinking of the motel, I said, "I wonder if they found them yet."

Roy knew exactly what I was talking about.

"I don't think so or we would have heard some kind of noise last night."

"Why did you think the cops wanted our room?"

Even though Dr. Becker was right there where he could see everything that was going on, Roy made one of those faces at me that implied, "Boy, you are really one dumb sister!"

"They wanted it for a lookout, stupid."

"What's that?"

"They plant some plain clothesmen there and then watch the place twenty-four hours to see if there is something fishy going on."

"How do they know there is going to be something fishy going on?" I asked, and the minute I did, I could tell Roy was going to explode.

"Well, how would I know?" he barked. "If they busted in a room, they must have some kind of lead on someone or something."

By now our voices were getting louder and louder, and Mom was getting both embarrassed and upset. But in her sweet preacher's-wife voice she said, "Please children, keep your voices down. Daddy and Dr. Becker are talking."

Now if we had been at home, Mother would have practically screamed, "Children, be quiet!" But here she could hardly do that, and Roy and I knew it.

After breakfast, we went back to our motel room and packed up our suitcases again. Dr. Becker led the way to our new house. The movers were supposed to arrive real early so Mother hoped everything would be there by now.

More and more I was less and less thrilled about this whole move. But by the time we got to our new house and I found that the bedroom that was to be

36

mine had just been redecorated, I got a little more excited. I guess the church had really done the whole house, but just about the only room I saw was mine. As I looked at it, I knew they had asked some teen-age girl how to decorate it because it was just perfect. Just exactly the way I would have done it if they had asked me.

That got me to thinking. Maybe there was a girl in our church who liked things I liked. Maybe God would give me a friend here after all. 'Course, she would never be the kind of friend that Susan Tanner was, but maybe, just maybe, there would be someone I could at least hang around with. Maybe she would be going to the same school we would go to and would introduce me to some of the other kids. For the first time in many weeks, I began to look forward to our new home and church in Lake Port.

Dad was walking Dr. Becker toward the front door when I came out of my bedroom.

"We appreciate all you've done for us," Dad was saying, and I wondered what that meant. Maybe the good doctor had slipped Dad a five and told him to take us to that pizza place. But that could hardly be. Nobody ever seemed to be thinking of pizza as often as Roy and I did. Somehow doctors just didn't think that way. They thought more about green and leafy vegetables, milk, and other things for a balanced diet. And preachers! Wow, they thought about a balanced diet as something to use for a sermon illustration! I couldn't even tell you how many times Dad had talked to us about the food we ate.

"Just like Mother fixes meat and vegetables and serves us milk," he would say, "so God wants us to care for our bodies in the right way."

Then he would go into a little sermon about how french fries and pop didn't make good bones in our bodies. Every single time, and I do mean every single time, Dad would quote the verse that said our bodies are the temples of the Holy Spirit.

It wasn't that I didn't believe it, because I did. I knew that was what the Bible said and I also knew that the Bible was God's Word and everything in it was true. It was just that—well, it was just that I liked french fries and pop even if they didn't make my bones strong.

Oh well, I had to admit that right now food didn't really matter. I was so pleased with my room that all I wanted was to find out who had helped decorate it. But before I could ask either Dad or Dr. Becker about it, the door bell rang.

"Hey, neato," Roy said, "Chimes."

Dad whirled and took one stern look at Roy. I

knew what he was thinking. He wished he could say, "Didn't I tell you to quit using that ridiculous word?" But he didn't make a single sound. I was pretty sure he would have if Dr. Becker hadn't been there. That made me wonder too. Why did people talk one way when they were alone with the family and another way when there were people around? Did other people talk to their kids that way? I was pretty sure everyone must have, but nobody wanted anybody else to hear them do it, I guess.

Dad went toward the door. But before he could put his hand on the door knob, the door swung open and a voice called out, "Hey, anybody live here?"

I recognized it immediately. It was my cousin Sam.

"Hey, Sam!" Roy cried out. But before I could say anything, my tongue just about flipped backwards down into my throat.

Sam? That was Sam? His hair hung to his shoulders, and I guessed that stubble on his chin was supposed to be the beginning of a beard. Right now it just looked like he had forgotten to shave for a couple of days.

Mother came dashing out of the kitchen when she heard us call out "Sam." Stunned, she blinked a couple of times as she looked at Sam's appearance.

"Where are Carl and—that is, your mother and

father?" she asked, trying to get her mind off what she was seeing.

Sam just grinned.

"The folks? They're missionaries in Latin America—remember?" Sam must have thought he was being very clever.

By now, Dad saw that Dr. Becker was wondering what was going on, so he apologized for the disruption and introduced them to each other.

"Doctor," he said, almost hesitantly. "This is my nephew. My brother and his wife are missionaries in Latin America. Sam is going to be staying with us for a while."

Dr. Becker held out his hand to Sam, but all the time his eyes expressed disbelief. I suppose he would have said something about Sam's appearance if he had not been so polite. Instead he said, "Hello, Sam. Welcome to Lake Port."

Dad looked at Sam. "I thought your folks were coming too." His voice showed disappointment, and I wondered if he was just wishing they were here to tell their son to clean up when he meets one of the church elders.

"They were coming," Sam said. "But I told them it was silly spending the mission's money when their furlough would be due in six months."

Mother raised her eyebrows, and I got to wondering if Sam really cared that much about the mission's money or if he just wanted to travel without his parents.

"I'm a big boy now, Uncle Will." He threw his head back in laughter, pushing his long hair away from his face.

I looked over to see how Roy was taking it all. I was pretty sure he wouldn't be saying "neato," but I really didn't know what he was thinking either.

Dr. Becker was still staring at Sam's beard; and as I turned to see what Dad was doing, I saw his hands moving nervously in and out of his pockets, something he had often scolded Roy for doing. Then I glanced over at Mom. She turned and walked back toward the kitchen. Shaking her head in disbelief, she said it again. "Oh my."

And that just about said it all.

5

An Unexpected Encounter

AFTER DR. BECKER had gone, we scurried around the house, trying to get some of the boxes unpacked and the house organized. Mother kept saying she could do it better if we weren't around, and I almost volunteered to get out of her way. I would have, but I didn't think Dad would appreciate it. Somehow he thought we all ought to pitch in and help and in that way get things straightened out that much faster. Mother tried to tell him that we were just in her way, but sometimes Dad acts pretty dense—at least when it comes to understanding that we don't have to work hard.

Sam didn't know what to do with himself. All he had was one small suitcase, and Mom wouldn't let him touch any of our things.

"Sam, have you eaten?" Mother finally asked when things quieted down a bit.

I sure didn't know why she asked that because there wasn't one speck of food in the house. I had already checked the refrigerator, and all I found were a couple of trays of ice cubes. I was pretty sure ice wouldn't do much to fill Sam's stomach if he was really hungry.

"Oh, sure. I had a big meal on the plane. Bacon, eggs, toast, orange juice—a good old American breakfast," he beamed.

Sam didn't say it, but I gathered that he didn't get that kind of food on the mission field. Well, actually, Sam wasn't exactly on a mission field. He was away at school most of the time his folks were out in the bush. They had been missionaries for so many years that I couldn't remember them ever doing anything else. Sam had wanted to stay home the last time they were on furlough, but Uncle Carl and Aunt Ethel had thought it would be better if he would take only his last year of high school in the States. That way he would be a little closer to them even if he would be many miles away at school.

While I was still thinking about Sam and the mission field, the telephone rang.

"Hey, our first call," I said as though it were a big event.

Dad answered it. "Oh. We did?" Dad said. "Yes, thank you. We'll be right there to pick it up."

I didn't know who had called, what we had done,

or where we were going to pick up what, but I could tell by the expression on Dad's face that whatever it was, it wasn't thrilling my dad too much.

"Who was that?" Mother asked when Dad put the phone receiver back on the cradle.

"The motel owner," Dad said with disgust. "You left your overnight case."

"*I* left it?" Mother said, raising her voice. "*You* were supposed to put it in the car."

"I asked Roy to take care of it."

"Me?" Roy shouted. "I thought you told me to take the big suitcase. That's the one I picked up."

While everyone else was making the rounds on who was supposed to have picked up the suitcase, I thought of something clever. Well, at least I thought it was clever. Making my voice sound something like Dad's, I said, "Forgetting those things that are be-hind—"

I thought maybe that would break up some of the bad tension. But all it broke up was Sam. He laughed while all the others looked at me like I was being terribly sacrilegious. I guess that's when Sam decided that he shouldn't be laughing either, so he changed the subject real quick.

"If you'll let me take your car, Uncle Will, I'll go get it for you."

44

For a brief minute that sort of shook Dad. I don't think he really trusted Sam to drive his car. As he looked at him, I could see a look in his eyes that silently asked, "How well do you drive?" But Dad had been trying to unpack his books and get ready for his first Sunday service at Lake Port Community Church. And chasing around a new town was his idea of a real waste of time.

"I'll go along and show Sam the way," Roy said so quickly that it disgusted me. Anybody would have known that Sam could read the street signs. He could have found the motel by himself. But Sam didn't seem to mind having Roy invite himself. So I thought I'd try the same trick. I knew Roy would object if I just plain asked to go along, so I had to come up with a better idea.

"Hey," I said as though I had a startling announcement to make. "It's almost time for lunch. Why don't we all go down there and then stop across the street for a pizza."

"I don't think pizza is much of a lunch," Mother said, wrinkling up her nose.

Dad seemed to agree.

"Well, then maybe just us kids can go," I added, hoping no one could tell those had been my thoughts from the beginning. I just didn't want Roy and Sam to get to go alone and me miss out on my favorite food.

"Shouldn't you stay here and help your mother?" Dad asked very seriously.

"Yeah, she should, Dad," Roy injected quickly.

"No, no, I'd just as soon work alone," said Mother. And I could have hugged her.

Roy wasn't too pleased to have me along, but Sam didn't seem to mind. Maybe cousins didn't get the same feelings about girls as brothers did. Anyway, before anyone could change their minds, I jumped into the back seat of the car and waited for the boys to come.

I could see Dad flip the keys to Sam, and then I heard him give a last-minute warning, "I hope you'll drive carefully."

"You don't have to worry about me, Uncle Will. I've driven since I was fifteen, and I've never had either an accident or a ticket," Sam boasted.

That seemed to please Dad and I think he decided maybe Sam wasn't so bad after all. But I got to thinking about where Sam had been driving. Maybe they didn't issue tickets on jungle roads. Oh, that Sam was a sneaky one.

After we left the driveway, Sam said, "I don't think your folks like my long hair or beard, do they?"

46

Roy shrugged. He didn't actually lie by just shrugging, because he was sure Mother hated it. He knew too Dad had just tolerated it in our other church. But one thing was sure, he had never let Roy's hair dangle too far over the ears.

"I think I'm going to get it cut," Sam volunteered. "To tell you the truth, it's a lot of bother; and if I go out for sports, I'll have to get it cut anyway."

"Sports!" Roy cried. "Are you going out for sports?"

"Sure hope so. At the government school where I went, they gave out letters for sports. I went out for basketball, baseball, track, and football."

I could see Roy's mind working pretty fast. If Sam was that good at sports, he could probably help him get into something at the Lake Port school. Oh, I knew that scheming brother of mine. He wasn't just sitting quietly thinking unless there was something he could get out of it for himself.

We had come to the street where the motel was located, and Sam turned into the drive leading to the entrance.

"We'll wait in the car," he said to Roy. "You jump out and get the case."

As Roy opened the door to the motel office, a

47

young, dark-haired fellow turned from talking to the manager and walked toward the open door.

Sam let out a yell.

"Carlos! That's Carlos!"

I turned around and noticed that Sam was looking into the motel office. Without another word he jumped out of the car and ran to the entrance of the building.

"Carlos!" I heard him say as the boy turned suddenly to face him.

"Samuel!" the dark-haired boy called back.

As the two of them threw their arms around each other, a paper flitted from Carlos' hand and blew across the driveway. I jumped out of the car to pick it up. Maybe it was something important that he would need.

I looked up at Sam and his friend and wanted to tell the boy that he had dropped the paper. But he and Sam were rattling away in Spanish, and I knew I wouldn't get a word in edgewise.

Suddenly the motel manager hurried out to the entrance. A strange look fell over his face. I wondered why. I was sure he didn't know Sam or this Carlos guy. And he had only met Roy and me the night before. Maybe he wished Roy had not been the one to come back to pick up the suitcase, after the

48

way he had spouted off about the cops and stuff last night.

I looked back at the paper I had picked up. I didn't really mean to read it, but there was no other place for my eyes to go since I didn't exactly want to stare at Sam and Carlos hugging each other. The writing was big and I felt my heart almost jump to my throat as I saw the words:

CARL—

I'LL HAVE TO GIVE YOU ANOTHER ROOM. NUMBER SEVEN WAS RAIDED LAST NIGHT.

BEN

I began to shudder. Was Carl the same Carlos that Sam was talking with? Was he the person the police had been looking for in room number seven last night? And how did Sam know him?

While I was standing there wondering all these things, the motel manager walked over to me, grabbed the paper from my hand and said roughly, "I'll take that."

6

The Suspicious Mr. Sinkey

FOR A MOMENT I trembled after the man had jerked the piece of paper from my hand. I looked up at him and saw that he wasn't smiling. The tag on his coat showed his name to be B. Sinkey. *The B. is for Ben,* I thought to myself. But I didn't dare ask him if I was right.

"It was blowing on the driveway," I said, pointing to the note he crumpled in his hand. "Carlos dropped it when he and Sam went into that clinch." I smiled as I said that.

The expression on Mr. Sinkey's face changed. Suddenly he was smiling too. "Oh, I don't think it came from him. I just saw it floating around and was going to come and pick it up. You know what they say about littering." He laughed loudly enough for both Carlos and Sam to hear.

Littering, my foot! I thought to myself. If I hadn't sneaked a look at that note, I might have believed him. But I *had* read it and I *did* know what it said. I wondered if Mr. Sinkey had seen me reading it. Right now all I knew was that this man was lying. And he had lied to us before. Last night when he had come to tell us about changing our room, he said it was because Dad was a preacher and he wanted to treat us special. We all knew that wasn't the truth. And now I was sure he was lying about the note too.

He looked over toward Sam and nodded in his direction.

"A friend of yours?"

"My cousin from Latin America."

"Latin America!" he said in surprise. "Did he know—this Carlos, or whatever his name is, from there?"

"I don't know. Is Carlos from Latin America?"

"Well—well, I would assume so, wouldn't you?"

"Maybe," I said. "Do you know Carlos very well?"

"Oh, no, I just met him a few minutes ago. He came in to register for a room."

"I hope you didn't give him number seven," Roy said, butting in on our conversation.

Mr. Sinkey bristled and then started to cough. When he could talk again, he looked at Roy.

"And what's the matter with number seven?"

Roy looked at the motel manager in surprise.

51

"Don't you remember? That's the one the cops tried to raid last night."

"Oh, yes, certainly."

When Roy first mentioned room number seven, I thought Mr. Sinkey was going to explode. He had coughed like something had gone down the wrong hole in his throat. That Roy! He could say the dumbest things and get himself into trouble without even trying. Why did he have to say that right now? It sure had seemed to get to Mr. Sinkey.

By now Sam and Carlos had finished talking and were coming toward us.

"Roy. Joy. This is my friend Carlos from Latin America. We went to the same school. Carlos, these are my cousins. They just moved into town this morning."

Carlos held out his hand.

"I have known Samuel for many year. He is very good football player."

Roy brightened considerably.

"Do you play football too, Carlos?"

The Latin teen shook his head.

"No, I am more a soccer player. But I am not good like Samuel here. He is like, what you say, professional."

"Do you live here?" I asked, wondering why he had come to Lake Port.

"Yes," he said. "I have been at this motel for several days."

I glanced over at Mr. Sinkey from the corner of my eye and wondered if he had heard what Carlos just said. I decided he had not since the expression on his face did not change.

But that was lie number three. Mr. Sinkey said Carlos What's-his-name had just now come in to ask for a room. Carlos said he had been here for several days.

Sam took his friend by the arm, and together they walked back toward the car.

"We've got to be going, or my uncle and aunt will wonder what happened to us."

"I hope we will be able to see each other again sometime," Carlos said. "Just having someone to speak Spanish with is so—so refreshing."

"Sure. Maybe we can take in some of the school football games," Sam said.

"Oh yes, you will be going to school here?"

"One more year. And if I'm lucky, maybe I can get all my classes in the morning. Maybe we can get some work together," Sam finished.

"I am already finding many workings here. But none of them make me rich so very fast."

Mr. Sinkey took a step or two closer to the car. I wondered why he wasn't in his office doing his motel work. It seemed strange that he had time to stand outside and talk with some people he didn't even know.

"If you write your parents," Carlos was saying, "Do not mention that you have seen me here. I have not told my people exactly where I am."

Sam laughed and slapped his friend on the back.

"How come, Carlos? Are you trying to dodge them?"

Carlos looked at Sam as if to ask what he meant.

"Dodge? Oh, that means trying to get away from someone."

This time Carlos laughed.

"Oh yes, I guess in a way I am. I want to make many American dollar before I tell them where I am staying. I want them to know that I do well here."

"OK, Buddy," Sam said. "I won't write about it. I'm not the greatest letter writer anyway. I don't suppose my folks will be getting too many letters from me." He put the key back into the ignition and started the car.

"But if you get any good tips on work—you know,

work where you don't have to work too hard, let me know."

Mr. Sinkey, who hadn't said a word since he had talked with me about Carlos, finally spoke up.

"Tips? Oh yes, Mr. Carlos, that's something everyone likes."

I thought that was a stupid thing to say. And why did he call him Mr. Carlos?

Sam laughed and turned to the motel owner. "His first name is Carlos. You'd never believe his last name."

But before Sam or anyone else could say anything more, or even before I could figure out why Mr. Sinkey didn't know that Carlos was the first name when he had just registered at the motel, Carlos opened the door to the back of the car and got in.

I scooted over to the other side quickly. What was going on?

"Say, why don't I go with you now to where you are living?" he said to Sam. "Then I will know where it is when I want to come and visit you another time."

Sam thought that was a terrific idea.

"Sure, why not," he said and began to pull away from the motel.

Roy stuck his head out of the window, "Thanks

for calling about our suit—" But before he could finish speaking, Mr. Sinkey had disappeared into the building.

"Now what happened to him?" Roy asked nobody in particular.

That's when it dawned on me that something very strange was going on. Why had Carlos jumped into the car so suddenly, and why had Mr. Sinkey managed to get out of sight so fast?

All at once I thought I knew.

Cruising up the street, not more than a block away, was a familiar blue car marked "Lake Port City Police."

7

Too Much Imagination?

I THINK EVERYONE REALIZED that something was sort of funny when Carlos jumped into our car so fast. And when Mr. Sinkey disappeared somewhere into the motel, Roy wrinkled up his forehead and looked over at Sam.

"Man, did he ever scoot away in a hurry. He's really a weirdo."

I was glad Dad wasn't here right now. He would never let us call people weird or stupid or dumb or things like that, even if we thought they were. He said everybody is made in God's image and we don't have any right to say things like that about God's creation.

Another reason I was glad that Dad was at home was that if I told him what I had been thinking about Carlos and Mr. Sinkey, he would have told me that my imagination was working overtime again. Sometimes he'd say that I let it run wild, and boy, it was really running right now. Was this Carlos guy in some kind of trouble?

The thing that really bothered me was that Sam had known him in Latin America, and I kept wondering if they had planned something while they were there and decided to meet right here in Lake Port. Was that why Sam had not wanted Uncle Carl and Aunt Ethel to come with him? Boy, if I was thinking right about all this, then I really was right about Sam being backslidden, too.

I looked out of the back window of the car in the direction of the motel and wondered about this sneaky-looking manager. Was he in it too? He sure seemed interested in Carlos. But the thing that bothered me the very most was us—how did we get mixed up in it all?

While Sam was driving back toward the house, Carlos was talking a mile a minute—Spanish, of course. Sam was the only one who could understand him, and if Sam was listening he sure wasn't answering much. I heard him say, "si" a couple of times, and the first time he said it, I thought maybe Sam was trying to tell us to look at something, so I turned and looked out the side window of the car. Then I remembered that "si" was "yes" in Spanish, so I quit looking.

"Are you sure you want to go back with us to my uncle's house?" Sam asked his friend. "He's a preacher you know."

"Si," Carlos said, "And so are your parents."

Sam didn't answer this time even though Carlos was talking in English now. Finally I could not stand it any longer.

"Carlos, were you trying not to be seen by that police car that went by the motel?"

When that statement plopped out of my mouth I thought both Sam and Roy were going to make us have a wreck. Sam turned all the way around and stared at me in the backseat, and Roy grabbed the steering wheel as he whirled around. Then both of them gazed at Carlos with a look of sympathy.

"What's that supposed to mean?" Roy asked, turning back to look at me again. His eyes were flashing with anger, and I knew that he thought I had really said an awful thing to Sam's friend.

"What police?" Sam asked, looking around the street on which he was driving.

Carlos laughed.

"Oh, this girl is making a funny joke. Why would I be running from the police? I have not even seen a policeman since coming to this town."

Carlos changed what I had said. I hadn't implied

59

that he was running from the police, just not wanting them to see him. If Dad or Mother had been here now they would have bumped my arm or hit me on the leg or done something that would have said, "OK, friend, you're talking too much."

But I still wasn't satisfied, so I kept asking more questions.

"How come Mr. Sinkey or whatever his name is, wanted to take you out of room number seven and give you a different room in the motel?"

This is when Roy really started raising his voice. In fact, he became very angry with me.

"Joy, for crying out loud. What are you doing?" He dropped his voice just a little, but I knew he wasn't through telling me off. "You know what Dad told you about making up dumb stories and letting your imagination run away with you. Man, you'd better quit that junk or—"

I didn't let him finish.

"But I saw it on the note," I said so seriously that Sam moved the rear view mirror and looked at me again.

"What note?" he asked. In a way he sounded disgusted, but at the same time I thought he really wanted to know what I was talking about.

"Remember when you pulled up at the motel

entrance and you first spotted Carlos, and you guys ran toward each other?" I said in one breath.

Sam remembered.

"So?"

"Well, when you guys hugged each other, this piece of paper flipped out of his hand." I pointed at Carlos. "I got out of the car to get it and I was going to give it to him as soon as you got done hugging."

Roy looked at me with a stare of disgust. I knew what he was thinking. Boys didn't hug, they just—well, they—well, all I could say is that Sam and Carlos hugged. That was all that there was to it.

"Then when Mr. What-cha-ma-callit came out from the motel, he grabbed the note away from my hand and crumpled it up. But I had already read it."

By now Roy was past the angry stage. He sounded furious.

"In the first place you're not supposed to read anyone else's notes. And in the second place, what did it say that was so bad?"

What a dumb brother! He tells me I wasn't supposed to read the note, and then he asks me what was in it.

All the time Roy and I had been spouting off at each other, Carlos had been just sitting there looking at us. I thought he would have defended himself if

I was accusing him of something wrong, but he hadn't said a word.

Sam looked over his shoulder, like he was trying to comfort his poor defenseless friend, but he didn't say anything more either.

Finally when there seemed to be a long enough break in the conversation, Carlos spoke up.

"Oh, you mean that note about changing rooms?" he asked.

I was surprised that he would even admit there was a note, let alone tell us about the content.

Roy looked at Carlos. Then he looked back at me and shook his head.

"Is that all? A note about changing rooms. Well, don't you remember that we had to change rooms last night too? And nobody made a federal case out of that."

Remember? Oh, I remembered all right. That was exactly what had made me start all this wild thinking.

Now Carlos was in a talking mood.

"I can explain everything." He moved forward, leaning on the top edge of the front seat as though he wanted to explain it to Sam.

"I have been living at this motel for a few days— maybe three, maybe four days. The motel man told me that there had been some trouble and the police had been there to look it over. So he thought I should not be near the room where they were searching."

"See!" Roy said, practically staring a hole through me. "The same thing happened to us. Hey, they must have a real racket going over at that place— moving people."

When Roy said "racket" I thought Carlos would crack his neck, he turned so fast.

I still wasn't satisfied with all the excuses.

"How come the motel manager told me that you had just come in a couple of minutes before we got there?"

Carlos' dark face turned crimson. For a minute there was silence in the car. Finally Sam came through with a reasonable explanation. "Maybe he meant that Carlos had just walked into the office for something right then."

"Why sure," Roy said. "For cryin' out loud, what are you trying to do to this guy? Don't you know he's a friend of Sam's?"

For a brief second I felt sorry for all I had said. Maybe I really was letting my imagination wander out of control like Dad had often told me. Maybe there really wasn't anything wrong. Maybe it just happened that the police had driven by just about the same time that Carlos decided he wanted to go to our house and visit with Sam. Maybe—

Roy wasn't through blasting me.

"Carlos, let me tell you something about that gal sitting next to you. She can make up some of the best mysteries you ever heard. I think she ought to write for television. She'd make a lot of money."

By this time the guys in the car were laughing it all off. But I wasn't laughing.

I didn't really think there was anything funny to laugh at. In fact, I thought it was a big problem. Right now I couldn't get anyone to believe me, but I would if there really was something wrong. I remembered something Dad had taught me long ago. "Whenever you have a problem," he had said, "and you feel no one understands you, remember God does."

I was quiet for a time, just talking with God, asking Him to help me so if there was something wrong I would know, or else tell me to apologize if it was nothing.

Roy turned around and looked at me once while I was praying to myself. I was sure he wondered why I wasn't arguing, but he didn't ask. All of a sudden I started humming "No One Understands Like

Jesus." Boy, it was a good thing He did, because no-body else was listening to me. Then I got a real calm feeling, like nothing really mattered. I knew God was going to take care of it. I didn't know how—I didn't even know what it was. I just knew He would do it. That's what Dad had taught us. A verse I had memorized came to me: "Trust in the Lord with all thine heart and lean not unto thine own understanding. In all thy ways acknowledge him and he shall direct thy paths."

We had only been in Lake Port about twenty-four hours and I had really managed to find trouble. That bothered me, because I thought moving to another city I could sort of start over with a clean slate. I had determined not to make up stories and exaggerate like I had before. And I had asked God to help me with it. If Mother had been here, I knew she would come through with, "Oh my!"

But I took a deep breath and whispered, "Oh, dear Lord," and I knew He was listening.

By the time we got in the area of home everyone had seemed to forget everything that happened or that I had practically accused Carlos of being on the police list. The boys had talked about Latin America, sports, school, and everything. As we turned to the street nearest to the house, I suddenly remembered that we were supposed to stop for lunch. That's when I really decided that nobody had taken lightly what I had said because of all the things that Roy would think of, it was lunch.

"Hey!" I called out. "We forgot to stop for pizza."

"Oh, brother," Sam said, and Roy groaned too.

"There is an eating place down this street," Carlos said pointing in the opposite direction of our house. "Ben and I were there last week."

"Ben?" Sam asked. "You mean you do know someone in this town after all? I wondered why you'd pick Lake Port."

"Ben, he is the man you met at the motel. He and I went to this place the day I first arrived in Lake Port."

Suddenly I realized that I wasn't hungry; not even for pizza. Ben something or other was the same man who called himself Mr. Sinkey. And he and Carlos did know each other. He sure wouldn't take a stranger out to dinner the first time he came to get a room in his motel.

The more I thought about this whole thing, the more disturbed I got. And the thing that bothered me the most was Sam. Had he known that Carlos was here? Was it all a put up? Maybe we had been included in their schemes. Maybe we were involved in a big mess, and maybe it would be better if I didn't say maybe, because right now it seemed pretty sure.

8

An Invitation to Stay

AFTER DINNER we pulled up in front of the house
and at exactly the same second Mother came out the
side entrance, a dust mop in her hand. I knew very
well what she had been doing and was a little surprised that she didn't come out to the car with a pail
and a scrub brush, telling me that she was ready for
me to help.

"I thought you got lost in this new town," she
said.

Sam spoke for all of us.

"Sorry, Aunt Joyce. It took a lot longer than I
thought. You see, I met a friend of mine from Latin
America."

He turned and faced Carlos.

"Carlos, this is my Aunt Joyce."

Carlos politely offered his hand. Just then Dad
came out the front door.

"Oh, you children finally got back."

Roy and I hated being called "children" and when

Dad said that, I wondered what in the world Sam must have thought. He was a lot older than we were.

"Uncle Will, I bumped into Carlos there at the motel."

Dad and Mom both seemed to like Carlos right away. They invited him to come into the house and that in itself was something. Usually when Mom was cleaning no one was allowed to come in until it was 100 per cent perfect.

"You know Sam's parents then," Dad said, stating a fact rather than asking a question.

"Si. They are missionaries in our country."

I looked over at Sam and then turned toward Carlos.

I wondered if he was going to say that Sam was a missionary too. But he said no more.

"Did you come to the United States with Sam?" Dad asked.

"Oh, no," Sam answered for his friend. "I had no idea Carlos was coming to the States, let alone be here at Lake Port.

"You mean to tell me you just bumped into each other?" Dad's voice showed that he thought it was unbelievable.

"Yeah, Dad," Roy added. "At the motel, the one we stayed at."

"Incredible," Dad said, shaking his head.

"And Dad, get a load of this," Roy continued, laughing so hard he could hardly finish his story. "Carlos stayed in room number seven this week. Wouldn't that have been a blast if he'd been there when the cops busted down the door?"

Dad looked at Roy and then at Carlos with a questioning look.

I was pretty sure Dad wasn't thinking what I was thinking. But boy, that just reminded me about everything I had—or thought I had seen.

"Are you living at the motel?" Mother asked.

"Si, for a few days. I am looking for another place soon."

"He's in this big old country all by himself," Sam added.

"It will not be so lonely now that I have spotted Samuel," Carlos added with a smile.

"Well, you shouldn't have to be paying big motel bills," Dad said. "Why don't you just spend the weekend here with us? That way you and Sam can have some time to get reacquainted. And next Sunday you can meet the young people from the church."

I just about swallowed my tongue. Of all the things I had been thinking about Carlos and Mr.

Sinkey, and now Dad invites Carlos to stay with us and even go to church.

"Sure," Sam said, "That would be great. You can share my room."

"Neato," Roy said before he thought. "I mean, that really would be fun. With two sports' pros in the house, maybe some of their talent will rub off on me and I'll have a chance at our new school."

Sam doubled up his fist and tapped Roy lightly on the arm.

"You've got a one track mind, man."

"Well, this will work out great," Roy added. "Carlos has to get out of his room anyway. Remember that manager told him he'd have to give him another room?"

"Well, one more trip back to the motel," Sam said.

"Why don't we wait and go back in the morning." Carlos added. "That is, if it is all right for me to stay here tonight."

"Why, yes," Dad said, "But you boys might just as well get out of Mother's hair for another hour or so."

I think when Dad first asked Carlos to stay with us, Mother could have put her tender little fingers around his size fifteen and a half neck. But now that she had had a chance to talk with Carlos a little, she seemed to be very agreeable. And Dad's idea to get them out of the house a little longer pleased her even more.

"If we go to this motel again," Roy said, "I vote for leaving Joy at home. She just makes up big stories and starts problems and things."

"I do not. I just read the note."

Mother and Dad looked at us, wondering what in the world we were talking about this time. Roy and I usually went round and round on things, and more than half of the time the folks didn't even try to figure us out. But this time I could tell by the looks on their faces that they really wondered how I could have managed to get into some situation before we even had our furniture unpacked.

Dad gave the car keys back to Sam.

"You fellows better go alone. I think Mother needs Joy to help her here."

Oh great, I thought to myself. *Another scrubbing party!*

"Sorry, girl," Carlos said, and he sounded so sincere.

"Yeah, sorry, Joy," Roy repeated. "Happy scrubbing to you and be sure you do a good job on my room." With that he dashed out the door.

Dad walked to the car with Carlos and Sam. He took a long look at Sam's hair and finally gave it a tug.

"Doesn't this get pretty warm?" he asked.

I thought Sam might get mad at that because he had already planned to get his hair cut. Now maybe he would get upset at Dad teasing him about it and decide not to do it.

"Don't worry, Uncle Will, I plan to get it cut this week." He shook his head, flipping his hair away from his face. "I want to go out for sports, and I have the feeling that they're going to tell me it'll get in the way."

Being the preacher he was, Dad came through with a fitting Scripture verse. "Let us lay aside every weight which doth so easily beset us," he quoted.

Carlos looked at Dad strangely and then turned and looked back at Sam.

"What did the 'father' say Samuel?"

"Oh, that was just something from the Bible," Sam said, trying to make it sound unimportant and at the same time trying to ignore the father title. With that they got into the car where Roy was waiting and drove away.

Dad came back into the living room, a look of surprise on his face.

73

"That boy didn't recognize a Bible verse and he even called me 'father,' as he would a priest."

"Isn't he from Carl's church?" Mother asked with surprise in her voice.

"Not on your life," I volunteered. "I doubt that Carlos has much to do with any church."

Mother flashed a quick answer.

"Whatever makes you say that?"

"Sam didn't meet him where Uncle Carl and Aunt Ethel are. He met him at the school he went to."

"By the way, Joy," Dad said, bringing up Roy's tattling statement. "Were you causing some sort of problem at the motel?"

"Oh, no, Dad, honest, I wasn't." I think the seriousness of my voice surprised my Dad. "It's just that I really don't think Carlos is—" my voice went off into nothing.

"Well, never mind that now," Mother broke in. "Let's get your room straightened out first. Then we can get the boys' rooms ready before they come back."

For once in my life I didn't feel like arguing when Mother told me to help her clean. All I could think of was that Mother and I would be there alone, and maybe I could tell her about what I had seen this afternoon. Her imagination was pretty much like mine and maybe, just maybe, she would understand.

As I went to the kitchen to pick up the pail and the scrub brush, I stood and stared into the bottom of the pail. I couldn't help but wonder if Mother and Dad were going to be sorry they had invited Carlos to spend the weekend with us.

Oh, I hoped I was wrong. Oh, how I hoped I was wrong. At that moment I knew I couldn't even share my thoughts with my mother. And that was a terrible, terrible feeling.

9

Two Empty Seats

SUNDAY MORNING at our new house was just like it had always been at Parsonage Hill. Everyone was chasing around the last minute to get ready for church. Everyone, that is, except Carlos and Sam.

When Mom knocked on their door to tell them breakfast would be ready in a couple of minutes, Sam called out to her.

"We're sleeping in, Aunt Joyce. We'll get a bite later on."

It was a good thing they couldn't see her look of shock.

"I knew they wouldn't go to church today," I said to Roy. "Carlos isn't the church type, and Sam is happy to find an excuse."

Roy refused to believe me.

"Sam promised Dad."

"Promises, promises. They don't mean anything to a couple of guys like Sam and Carlos."

"You don't know either one of them. So how can you talk like that? They'll be there," Roy said confidently.

"I'll betcha they won't."

A few minutes before we were ready to leave for Sunday school, Sam stuck his head out of the bedroom door.

"Don't wait for us," he said. "We'll come later—for church."

"How will you get there?" Dad asked. "There's only one car."

"We'll hoof it," Sam said. "Remember, we've hiked around the Andes. A few blocks to church won't hurt us."

He laughed and closed the door again.

I looked at Roy in my best I-told-you-so manner but said nothing at the time. I knew Mother and Dad didn't want us fussing before church.

It was strange, meeting so many of the church kids all at once, but everyone in our Sunday school class seemed real nice. I got to meet Delores, the girl who had decorated my room, and I told her how much I liked it. As I talked with her, I thought again that this might be the person who would be most like Susan Tanner. Maybe God was going to answer my prayer and give me a friend right away.

She turned and faced a tall boy standing nearby. "Hey Brad, meet Joy Sparton."

I looked up at Brad, all the time pretending in my mind that he was David Tanner. Brad must have been a year or so older than David and he had a lot more pimples, but otherwise they were built alike. Brad had brown eyes, just like David, and his curly hair kept falling into his face, just like David's did.

When the bell rang ending Sunday school, Delores asked me to sit with her in church. I thought that would automatically include Brad, but much to my surprise he and Roy took off for the opposite side of the church as Delores and I found seats near the back.

Brad and Roy could have taken the two empty seats next to us, but I just knew that if Brad had considered that possibility for even one second, Roy would have suggested that they sit on the opposite side. That brother of mine could be so sneaky at times!

I looked all over the church to see if Sam and Carlos had come in, but just as I thought, they were nowhere in sight. I knew Sam's promises had been just a lot of talk; they never intended to show up. I was sure of that.

I stared over at Roy until I finally got his attention

and with exaggerated motion I lipped the words, "I told you so." If we hadn't been in church, Roy probably would have made a face or something, but instead he just raised his eyebrows as if to say, "So?"

Even now as the organist was finishing her prelude, I kept thinking about Sam. I couldn't really prove that he was in trouble, but the more I thought about it, the more convinced I was that something was terribly wrong.

As Dad stood and raised his hands for the congregation to stand and sing the doxology, two people brushed past Delores and me and slid into the two empty seats beside us. Sam—and Carlos! I almost shouted it aloud.

I really didn't want to look in Roy's direction, but my eyes were drawn that way and I saw the smirk on his face. "I told you so!" Roy lipped. His message came across the sanctuary loud and clear.

I gave my hymn book to Sam when the first song was announced, but neither he nor Carlos sang a note. They had shown up at the service to please Dad, but they certainly didn't intend to take any part, I was convinced.

When it was time for the sermon I settled back in my seat, sure that whatever Dad was about to preach that day would be something that I had heard in our other church. After all, these people would never have heard the sermons he preached there, so it just made sense that he would repeat something.

Well, it may have made sense to me, but not to Dad. He had a brand-new message, one that I had never heard before. And boy, did he preach. For a moment I wondered if he thought he was talking to a bunch of people in a rescue mission. He talked about sin and forgiveness and Jesus' death for all men. If I had been a sinner like I was sure Carlos was or a backslider like Sam, I would have been terribly under conviction. But when I looked at them out of the corner of my eye, it seemed as though nothing was getting through. Carlos had spent most of the hour looking at his watch, and Sam just looked disgusted—or maybe uneasy.

When the service was finally over, and Dad was just about to pronounce the benediction, Dr. Becker, the chairman of the church, stood up and announced a surprise dinner in the church basement to honor the new pastor and his family. Carlos uttered a groan of some kind and looked at his watch again. Sam said something to him, but since it was in Spanish I could not understand it.

Then in English Carlos said, "I'm leaving."

"You've got to eat, so what's the diff?" Sam said. But Carlos shook his head vigorously.

The line toward the door moved slowly as everyone took their time to visit with their pastor. Carlos was getting edgy and nervous, and when he finally got to the entrance where Mom and Dad were standing, I heard him tell Mother not to look for him tonight.

"I have—an—appointment," he spoke hesitantly, and it wasn't because of his uncertain English either.

Appointment! I thought to myself. He was new in town. How could he have an appointment—and on Sunday?

Sam had heard him too, and I could see the distress signals appearing on his face.

"Carlos, wait for me. I'm going along," he said. But before either of us could get out of the line, Carlos had made a mad dash for the entrance. I followed him as quickly as I could and saw only at a distance where he was headed. A station wagon parked at the far end of the drive began to move up, and Carlos ran to it and jumped in. I strained to see who else was in the car but could only see the driver. The driver! It was Mr. Sinkey, the man from the motel!

As the car pulled away with a jerk, I suddenly felt

sick. If there was one thing I could not do right now, it was go back to the church for the fellowship dinner. How could I meet a bunch of new people at a time like this? Instead, I walked hurriedly toward the parking lot, all the time wondering if Mother would forgive me if I just sat it out in the car. I opened the door and slumped into the back seat, my mind in a big whirl.

"Oh dear Lord," I prayed, and that was all that would come out.

All of this couldn't be my imagination. There was something wrong. I just didn't know what it was.

10

Nabbed by the Police

I KNEW MOTHER AND DAD would be looking for me at the church, and I would have a lot of explaining to do later on. But right now I could not go in and attend the fellowship dinner. It would mean that I would not get to meet some of the kids, but right at this moment even that did not seem to matter. Before I could collect my thoughts and decide what I should do about telling Mother where I was, the car door opened and Sam jumped in behind the wheel.

"Joy," he cried. "Get out of here! I've got to have the car."

"Where are you going?" I asked.

"Never mind. Just get out of here."

"You're in trouble, Sam. And I'm not leaving."

"This is an emergency. Now get out!" His voice rose loudly.

By this time I was becoming more inquisitive.

"Where did you get the keys?"

"Your dad gave them to me. I told him it was urgent."

"And he just let you have them with no explanation?"

"Joy, I don't have time to argue, get out of the car."

I refused to move.

"If I don't go now I'll miss Carlos."

"So you are in trouble with Carlos," I stated flatly. "Mr. Sinkey, too?"

Sam looked at me in surprise, but for an answer he started the car and backed out of the parking lot.

"I've got to get to Carlos before he does something stupid."

"Before *he* does something stupid! What about *you?*" I barked.

"Just sit down and be quiet. There's enough trouble without you adding to it."

There. Sam all but admitted that he was in deep trouble.

The more he talked, the faster he drove.

"Sam, you're going over the speed limit."

"Right now I can't help it."

"The cops will get you."

"I'll have to take that chance."

Sam sounded so serious I almost felt sorry for him.

Oh, how I wished I knew what was wrong. Maybe I could help him. Then the thought occurred to me that if I could manage to keep Sam from arriving wherever he was going, he probably wouldn't be involved. But how?

By now I was pretty sure we were headed back to the motel. We were going in that direction.

The needle on the speedometer kept going higher and higher. Maybe Sam, Mr. Sinkey, and Carlos had agreed to pull some job and now Sam thought they were running out on him.

Then an idea came to me. If Sam continued at this high rate of speed, surely one of the policemen patroling in this area would pick up the chase, stop him, and that would delay his going to the motel to meet Mr. Sinkey and Carlos.

Silently I began to pray: *Oh God, Sam is in some kind of trouble. Will you please send a cop to see him speeding because that way he'll be stopped and not be involved in whatever they have planned for today.*

Before I could even say "amen" Sam blurted out. "Oh, God, don't let me be too late."

I thought it was pretty nervy of Sam to ask God for help in whatever they were planning to do. It was— Well, it seemed wrong, but I said nothing.

With exaggerated recklessness, Sam whirled into the motel driveway, drove around to the back side of the building and jerked to a sudden stop beside room number seven. My stomach felt like it was up in my throat. There in front of the door stood the station wagon that had picked up Carlos at the church.

"I'm in luck," Sam said. "They're still here."

"Please don't go in, Sam," I cried. But he refused to listen to me. He jumped out of the car, leaving the door open in his haste.

Then knocking on door number seven Sam called, "Carlos, let me in. Carlos. This is Sam."

But before Sam could knock a second time, two uniformed men came up behind him, took him by the arm, and stepped toward an approaching car marked "Lake Port City Police," which had come suddenly around the corner.

"Okay, friend," one of them said. "This is it. The end of the trail."

Sam looked genuinely surprised.

I watched as they led my cousin to the car, more frightened than I could ever remember being in my whole life.

As I watched, four other officers approached room

number seven and kicked in the door, entering in force.

I looked back to see what was happening to Sam.

"And who's the little girl?" one of the officers said. "Better take her along." Any other time I would have resented being called a little girl, but no time in my life did I feel more like one than I did right at that moment.

The policeman came to Dad's car and got me. "Just for a few questions," he said. Before I fully realized what was happening, I had been led to the back seat of the police cruiser and was seated next to Sam.

"Joy," Sam whispered. "I told you not to come. I was afraid there would be trouble."

"Sam, what have you done?" I asked, loudly enough for him to hear but hopefully not loudly enough to let the police officers get something on him.

He just shook his head.

All at once I remembered that Mother, Dad, and Roy were having dinner at our new church and meeting the people that Dad was to pastor.

The new church. Oh, what would the people think when they read in the morning paper "Preacher's Daughter Arrested in Raid"?

Without warning I broke into uncontrollable sobs. I had done it already. Dad had been the pastor of the Lake Port Community Church exactly one day and I had already caused a scandalous problem. I had ruined his ministry.

11

Sam Comes Clean

EXACTLY WHAT HAPPENED between the time Sam and I were taken to the police station, and Dad, Mother, and Roy arrived, I don't really know. I tried to find out who called them, but in the confusion nobody heard my question. They were almost as upset as I was. I remember they said something about coming in Dr. Becker's car, since Sam had ours, and that made me feel really awful again.

It seemed like Sam and I had been there for about ten hours, but I guess it had only been an hour or so. A big police officer came into the room where we were all sitting.

"Well, I guess you're clean," he said, nodding his head toward me. "You can go with your parents. But we may need you for questioning later."

Questioning about what? I couldn't believe it. Dad turned and talked with Dr. Becker, and that was the first that I realized he was in the room. "I'll go find a telephone," Dr. Becker said.

89

While he was out, Dad told the officer that we would not be leaving until an attorney could arrive.

"Sam is living with us," he said. His voice cracked almost as much right now as it did the day he was praying before we left Parsonage Hill. "We're responsible for this boy."

"Do as you please," the police officer said, "but we've got some more checking to do on him."

"That's fine," Dad said. "We'll just stay here until our attorney arrives."

"OK. It'll be another thirty minutes before we book him."

I took another look at Sam, and I was sure he was going to break out in tears just any minute.

"Oh, Uncle Will," he said. "They'll never believe the truth."

Dad sat down next to him.

"Why don't you try telling it to me."

Mother left the chair on the other side of the small room and sat down on the bench next to Sam and me.

"Is Joy mixed up in this some way?" she asked anxiously.

Sam seemed surprised with her question.

"Joy? No, she just happened to be in the car."

Mother whirled in my direction. I knew she was

90

upset. "Why would you go to the car when you knew they were having this dinner for us at the church?"

Words wouldn't come out. All I could do was shrug my shoulders.

Dad came to my relief. "That's not important now."

"Joy saw Carlos get into Sinkey's car," Sam interrupted.

"What?" Dad asked, not seeing any connection.

By this time Roy looked in my direction and spoke his first words. "You mean you were right about Carlos and Mr. What's-his-name?"

If I hadn't felt like crying, I would have said, "I told you so," but right then I couldn't be mean even to my brother.

Sam took a deep breath and started telling Dad the whole story. "Carlos got in trouble about a year ago at school. They suspected him of selling drugs, but they couldn't prove anything so he just quit school. I never saw him again until the other day at the motel. That was really a fantastic coincidence."

Sam stopped long enough to wipe the perspiration from his forehead.

"When I first saw him, I forgot all about the drug thing—until last night. I started asking too many questions and to keep me quiet Carlos talked Sinkey

91

into cutting me in on the deal. I knew I could never really do it. They had decided that the two of us living with a preacher was the best coverup they could have. But they got itchy for time and Sinkey made arrangements to move the stuff today. He was supposed to pick up Carlos at the church right at noon—"

"And I preached a little too long and threw them off schedule," Dad finished for him.

Sam nodded. "Your sermon got to me, and I knew I'd have to do something. I tried to get Carlos to stay for the dinner. I knew if he did, Sinkey would have to handle the deal alone and Carlos might get off a little easier too. But he wouldn't hear of it."

The police officer who was in the room with us kept taking notes. And Sam turned and faced him.

"I don't suppose anyone will believe this story, but it's the truth."

Dr. Becker came back and a tall, graying man with him.

"Looks like the Lord was a step ahead of us," he said. "Attorney Crandall was in the building for someone else. I asked him to come in here, too—we needed him right away."

"You won't need him any longer," said the police-man who had first brought us in. I hadn't even seen him come back. "We've checked out this story and the South American kid tells us exactly the same thing."

Dad brightened. "You mean, Sam is free to go?"

"Sure," the officer said. Then he turned and faced Sam. "I would like to give you a piece of advice, son. Be a little more careful in the friends you pick. These jokers almost got you mixed up with a million-dollar drug ring. They figured they could use Carlos to smuggle in drugs, and nobody would suspect the stuff was coming into a small town like Lake Port. Then they could channel it out to larger cities."

"Million dollars?" Roy said. "Man!"

Dad shook his head.

"And to think we can hardly get money for the missionaries serving the very country where this boy came from."

He had tried to whisper that to Mother, but we all heard it.

Attorney Crandall turned to Dr. Becker. "Well, there's no point in my sticking around."

He walked over to Sam and shook his hand. "You'd better get down on your knees and thank your Maker that you weren't involved in this one," he said. "The local police have been on it for more than eight weeks, not to mention government agents who have been investigating the international activities. I was just talking with the Latin boy, and he told me how he met Sinkey about a year ago, right after he left school. Sinkey offered him a lot of money. So now he's in quite a mess."

Dr. Becker shook hands with Dad and then walked to the doorway with the lawyer.

"Well, I don't see anyone who is sick, so I guess you don't need me either."

"How will we get home?" I asked. "Our car is at the motel?"

Roy slapped his hand across his forehead. "Oh, no, not another trip to that motel."

"Not for me," I said. "Someone else can go along to get the car."

The police officer entered the room again.

"Reverend, if you're looking for your car, you'll find it on the parking lot. It was brought in for checking."

" 'Before ye ask—' " Dad started.

"I knew it," I said. "I knew Dad would finish up with a Bible verse. He has one that fits everything."

Sam continued to stare at the floor. "He'd better have one for a backslidden guy who wants to come clean with the Lord," he said.

I looked up at Dad to see if he would react when Sam called himself a backslider.

"That's the point you need to come to," Dad said. Then he took out his Bible and started showing Sam some verses.

Mother was crying. Roy looked more serious than I had seen him for a long time. And me? I went over to the other corner of the room and thanked the Lord for leading us and Sam to Lake Port. This week both of our houses had had a revival, Sam had had a revival, and maybe it would even spread to our new church. It had already made me come closer to the Lord.

"There is something I have to do," Sam said as we were finally leaving the police station. Dad gave his long hair a tug just like he had done before.

Sam got Dad's point. "Oh yeah, that too," he laughed. "I decided several days ago that was coming off."

Dad was a little embarrassed. He was sure Sam had been talking about getting a haircut.

"How many rooms are there in your new house?" Sam asked. I thought he was changing the subject.

I started listing them. "Kitchen, living room, dining room, and four bedrooms."

95

"Perfect," Sam said. "That makes my room number seven. I want to stop and get a numeral to hang on my door to remind me what it took to get straightened out with God."

And wouldn't you know it. Dad got the last word in again. "You're right, son," he said, and I could tell Sam was pleased to be called son. "The Bible tells us that number seven is perfect."